Shoı

LOVE &
ENTANGLEMENT

By
ANDY HOUSTOUN

Andy Houstoun is a philosophy teacher. He has had short stories published in a variety of magazines based in Great Britain, Australia and the USA, and has won two short story writing competitions. He lives in England with his wife and four children.

ISBN   979871008761

Thanks to all those at the Scribophile writing community who critiqued my early versions of the stories included in this book. Special thanks to Kathy Whipple, Antonia Rachel Ward, Curtis Bass, Anna Britton, Erin Hacket, EZ Linus, Jennifer Ostromecki, and Lisbeth Rivers. To the publications who had faith in my writing. To my family and friends for their encouragement: Josh, Dan, Zac, Si, Danola, Pete, Nic, 'Rudegirl' Rudie, Jase, Pete H, Zoe, Edie, Dustbunny, eris, Dave and Mazza. To those who inspired these stories: Emily Bronte, Thomas Hardy, Robert Smith of The Cure, Prince Rogers Nelson and Carol 'Blondie' Martin.

Contents:

Dedicated to Blondie.

Introduction

These stories were written during the Covid-19 lockdown of 2020. Originally, they were published in my book 'How to write short stories of Love & Entanglement', which contains commentaries ono how each story came to be, along with tips on how to get published.

This contains just the stories themselves.

'Waiting For Lulu At Wuthering Heights' was first published by Nauseated Drive in 2020. It was also published by Expat Press, and Adelaide literary magazine.

1. Waiting For Lulu At Wuthering Heights

Wordcount: 1, 762

"If all else perished, and he remained, I should still continue to be; and if all else remained, and he were annihilated, the universe would turn to a mighty stranger." - Wuthering Heights by Emily Brontë

I'm in The Wuthering Heights pub. I know, it's a shameless exploitation of the novel's title, but Lulu and I didn't care when we stumbled across this place in the early nineties. We liked the way it blatantly took advantage of its location on the edge of the remote Haworth moorland. We had dinner here before we set off into the open country with our tent and camping equipment.

Tonight though, I'm finishing my meal alone. I undo the top button of my shirt and release the pressure around my neck. I remove my Anglican clerical collar and place it on the table in front of me. Heavy snow has left the place empty. I'm the only customer tonight. I look towards the door, half expecting Lulu to walk in although it's highly unlikely. It's been eight years since I saw her.

I reach into my shirt pocket for a picture of her, taken in her student house in Birmingham. Her eyes stare back, wild and dark. Her pale skin is unblemished, with naturally pink cheeks. Blonde hair cropped short at the back, long at the front, hangs down to her jawline on one side. She changed hair colour frequently, but blonde suited her best. She's wearing a T-shirt from the Cure's Brixton Academy gig. Robert Smith's face is stretched across her chest, and at the bottom in red are the words: 'MIXED UP'. Behind her, scrawled over the walls in black ink, are verses of her poetry. She never stopped writing: in notebooks, on scraps of paper, on her hands, wherever she was, whenever she thought of it. She even wrote one on the back of this photo. I study the familiar words:

It's a picture of a house I built burning in my head,

It's a picture of a little boy bouncing on a bed,

It's a picture of a little girl bouncing by his side,

It's a picture of a daddy who may as well have died.

I turn it back over. There's a white fold line across the middle of the photo, but it's the only picture I have. I place it on the table next to my dog-collar.

Outside, snowflakes tumble down in ever-changing courses. Fleeting shapes fall and disintegrate on the glass before my eyes can catch them. More drift down against the winter landscape and I'm lost in memories again.

The first time I saw her was on my nineteenth birthday. I was in The Jug of Ale with my mate, Coddy. It was crowded; music thumping, lights flashing, everywhere the cacophonous din of laughter and chatting.

"Hey, Dan." Coddy nudged me, pointing to a girl on the dancefloor. "What do you think of her?"

I wasn't sure who he meant. Most of the girls

looked the same to me - short skirts and white stilettos.

"Yeah...she looks all right," I said.

It wasn't my kind of venue. I spent most of the night slowly nursing a pint of Guinness while Coddy did his best to impress any female who would listen to him. He'd managed to speak to a girl with long dark hair.

"So, what do you do?" she asked him.

"I'm an astronaut," he said, with his typical straight-faced confidence.

Then I saw Lulu. She walked up to the bar and stood inches from me. She wore a purple, knee-length dress with Doc Marten boots, but what drew me to her were her eyes. They were dark, glistening with life.

***

"Your bill, sir!"

The waiter places my bill on the table. Two men stand by the door, ready to lock up for the night. A glance at my watch tells me it's midnight. I apologize for keeping them, put my collar and photo in my pocket, and settle up. I step outside. It's stopped snowing and the wind has died down. Everything is white.

I pull my coat collar tight around my neck and wander along the path towards the heath, the inspiration for Emily Brontë's tragic love story. 'Wuthering Heights' was Lulu's favourite book.

Last time we were here it was under cloudless blue skies. I remember sitting outside our tent in the long grass surveying the endless moors, breathing the sweet warm air.

'Lovesong' by The Cure came on the stereo she had brought. I pulled her to her feet, and we danced. I said to her: "When you hear this song, think of me." I wanted to ask her to marry me there and then, but I was scared of being turned down.

Instead, I asked, "Do you think we'll still be together in ten years?"

"Maybe." She smiled, amused at my question.

And then, to try and ensure we didn't ever lose contact, I came up with this ridiculous idea: "Let's meet back here on my thirtieth birthday, whether we are or not. Midnight."

"Okay." She looked deep into my eyes and smiled.

I held the side of her face in my hand and reached towards her. Our lips touched. Tongues. Two souls merged; the outside world non-existent. Bodies touched; stirred.

***

A single snowflake lands on my nose. Then another. I look into the night sky as the snow starts to fall again. I pull back my coat sleeve and look at my watch. It's a quarter past midnight. I wander further down the lane.

"Like the eternal rocks beneath." That's how Lulu once described her love for me, and I felt the same. I'd never met anyone so fearless and unpredictable, yet introspective and deeply thoughtful. She studied Art, while I read Theology. We started going out after lectures, drinking and smoking together, talking into the early hours, spending every available moment with each other.

I walk through the falling snow, along a dim, deserted path in the direction of the rock face, close to where we camped. From the gate on my right, the lane slopes towards the open countryside. I sink up to my calves in soft, fresh snow. All I can hear is my own breathing and the light crunch of each step as I move forward.

Lulu was brought up in a Catholic orphanage on the west coast of Ireland. She didn't talk about her childhood much. All she said was that she'd been abandoned when she was six years old. She hated the thought of being left by anyone again; she told me she preferred not to get too close to people.

I arrive at a steep bank and the snow slides away in clumps. I grab a branch above my head and a dusting of white powder falls, but I've made it. I'm in an open space with a view of endless hills. I stand for a long time, taking it all in, looking for any sign of life on the beautiful, desolate moor.

She gave no explanation when she left, except that she needed to get her head straight. A week afterwards, I received a poem from her in the post, along with a note saying she was staying with an aunt in

Ireland. A few weeks after that, the lease ran out on my house. I tried everything to get in touch with her, but no-one could help. The university wouldn't provide me with any information, and no-one knew her home address, or even which village she was from. I never heard from her again. I spent a few months drinking myself into a numb haze until I realised I was better off getting my life back on track, training for the ministry, helping all those other brokenhearted people.

I've been the rector at St Matthews in Ayr for three years. None of the leadership or parishioners know anything about Lulu. I take a deep breath. Tonight, I hope to put old ghosts to rest. The air is crisp and still. Nearby branches crack as they strain under the weight of fresh snow. I stand motionless on the moor, listening.

A memory comes to mind. A tree we discovered here. It had been struck by lightning. All that was left was the remains of the trunk; the top brown and charred.

Lulu took out a penknife. It was about five centimeters long with a shamrock on the side. "This is the only thing I had from my mum," she told me. "It's not good for much but I use it for my art sometimes."

She crouched in the grass and carved into the trunk:

'Lovesong

Think of me

Always'

***

I'm not far from it. I step forward.

Around the side of a hill is the towering rock face we climbed. It was at the top that Lulu and I held each other, surrounded by endless countryside. I stand motionless, absorbed by the familiar sight, and it feels like she's here with me.

Another memory unfolds. Something she said to me. A Brontë quote. What was it? I close my eyes to concentrate. There was a moment when Lulu slipped from my arms and looked straight at me:

"Be with me always - take any form - drive me mad! Only do not leave me in this abyss, where I cannot find you!"

I open my eyes. The seriousness of her face when she said it. And yet here I am, back on the heath, unable to find her.

Praying feels pointless tonight. I reach into my coat pocket and take out a small bottle of Glenlivet. There's a crack as I twist off the cap. I hold the bottle to my mouth and take a generous gulp. The acrid taste of scotch burns the back of my throat. My eyes are warm with tears and I throw the bottle as hard as I can onto the heath. It lands with a quiet thud and disappears into the snow.

I stumble backwards a moment and through blurred vision, I see the burned-out tree. Such a distinctive sight. One side is covered in snow and the other untouched. I walk towards it and see the familiar words:

'Lovesong

Think of me

Always'

They've faded but are still visible. I run my fingers over the indentations and reach into my pocket. I take out Lulu's penknife. The only possession she owned that belonged to her mum.

A warm tear

rolls

down

my

cold face.

THE END.

'Lovesong' was 'Short Story of the Month' in the Australian magazine The Writing Quarter in July 2020.

2.

Lovesong

Wordcount: 1, 380

A pound coin

        clatters

             down

                the slot.

I scroll through the song choices of the old jukebox, and punch in 6-2-4.

A seven inch of The Cure's 'Lovesong' moves into position. The tonearm slides across and there's a crackle as the needle settles into the grooves.

A distorted guitar chord erupts from the speakers into the empty pub, and the familiar driving rhythm starts. The church-like organ, the bouncing bass, and the jangly guitar; churn up feelings that stir my gut.

I'm in The Wuthering Heights, a pub Dan and I visited in the early nineties. I go back to my seat and glance around the room.

It still has the same decor: lead-framed windows and ornate mirrors; paintings of the Yorkshire landscape in gilt frames. The smell of real ale and stagnant smoke.

I'm twenty again.

I stare at the door and imagine Dan walking in. I haven't seen him for years.

As 'Lovesong' plays on, I take out a letter. I found it in the pocket of this old coat when I put it on this morning. I planned to send it years ago. I look at my familiar handwriting:

"Dear Dan,

I'm so sorry.

I shouldn't have left you the way I did.

My feelings were becoming too intense, and I couldn't handle them.

I know I should have explained things better, but I was struggling so much. At the time it was easier to just..."

Tear stains distort the next letters and that's where it ends. I didn't even know I still had it until this morning.

Things were so different the last time we were here. We camped out on the moor. I remember every moment of it.

'Lovesong' came on the stereo that I brought along. Dan pulled me to my feet, and we danced, close. He looked into my eyes. "When you hear this song, think of me."

Then he paused and asked: "Do you think we'll still be together when we're in our thirties?"

"Maybe." I smiled.

"Let's meet back here on my thirtieth birthday, no matter what. At midnight."

I was hesitant. It was a crazy idea, but I said: "Okay."

A glance at the clock behind the bar tells me it's ten past twelve. There's no sign of Dan. It dawns on me that midnight could mean the turn of midnight first thing in the morning, or it could mean now - the night of his birthday.

Is it possible that he's already been? He might have gone straight to the place where we camped.

I gather my coat and step outside into the cold night air. Heavy snow has kept everyone away. There's not a sound except for the faint whisper of snowflakes landing all around me. The moon is big and bright.

I pull my hat down over my ears and trudge down the lane in the direction of where we pitched our tent. In the silence, as I set off, the crunch of my footsteps is deafening.

We met at university. He was different than the other guys. Contemplative. Reflective. A theology student, with a love of art and alternative music. Slim, with dark hair and green eyes, he lived in the attic of a Victorian house in a rough part of Birmingham. I remember the first time I visited. We had been spending a lot of time together and I had been interested to see his place. His room, full of canvases and books, intrigued me. Titles like 'Searching For God Knows What' and 'What's So Amazing About Grace?'. We ate together and shared a bottle of wine.

"Where are you from?" He asked me.

"Limerick."

"Sounds nice."

"Not really. I was brought up in a Catholic orphanage."

He looked at me with interest and I continued: "My dad left us when I was six. My mum didn't cope very well, and they took me off her a few months later. I didn't want to go, but they dragged me, kicking and screaming." I laughed at the thought of my six-year-old self so passionate and determined.

"Have you seen your mum or dad since then?"

"I don't think they'd be interested. All I know is I don't want to be left by anyone again. I prefer not to get too close to people." I downed the rest of my drink in one. "I'm no good, Dan. I'm no good for anyone. My mum told me; the nuns told me. It's all I ever heard." My voice broke and I looked down.

I felt his hand on my shoulder. He moved the glass away from me and touched my face. Our lips touched, and for a moment, nothing else mattered.

***

Snowflakes begin to fall like confetti as I walk along the deserted path, and more memories unfold.

"How do you know if you've found the person you want to marry?" I asked him one evening. We were both working on paintings in his room. His, a self-portrait with a dark, industrial background. Mine, an image of myself without hair, curled into the foetal position.

He looked up. "If it feels right, I guess."

"But what if you're not sure? How do you know?"

"Maybe it takes a while?"

***

I hear the muffled sound of voices and a television from inside a farmhouse as I pass by. A lantern hanging from the stone wall of the building glistens in the cold night air. The noise from the house dies away as I walk on.

When I left Dan, I told him I needed to get my head straight. I went back to Ireland and stayed with my aunt. Spent months working on paintings and poetry. Hardly left my room. I wrote to him. I kept writing for months but never heard back. I don't blame him. He was probably fed up with me. Maybe he found himself a nice sensible girl.

I stop for a moment and stand motionless, looking at the distant hills covered in thick snow. The moon is hidden behind a thick streak of cloud and my mind wanders back to yesterday morning:

"Where is it you're off to?" my aunt asked.

"Birmingham."

"Isn't that where you were at university?"

"That's right."

"What are you going back there for?"

"Just to visit an old friend."

She paused and then said: "Have you ever thought at all about settling down, Lulu?"

I smiled and sighed. "There was someone once, but it didn't work out."

"Have you considered dating anyone else? Rob's been asking after you a lot. He's a handsome man and he'd make a lovely husband." She peered over her glasses.

Rob was a family friend. He was sweet, but I couldn't lead him on with Dan still on my mind.

I shook my head. "I'm not ready."

***

Moonlight shines through the clouds and my eyes become accustomed to the light reflecting off the heath. Apart from black shadows under bushes, everything seems as bright as daylight. Then I hear a faint thud and feel a chill on my neck. I listen intently. I can sense someone near. Close behind me. Maybe two meters away. Maybe closer. I'm too scared to turn. A rustle. Someone out walking their dog, perhaps? Or is it just the sound of winter on the moors?

"Dan?"

I turn, but there's not a soul for miles. It's stopped snowing.

I take out an MP3 player and find our song. I put the headphones in my ears and press play. That desperate guitar-chord. I close my eyes and lose myself in the pulsating rhythm and Robert Smith's melancholy voice.

When I open my eyes, all I can see is a desolate landscape.

"Don't leave me in this abyss," I whisper.

I turn and see a tree I recognise. It had been struck by lightning which gave it an unusual shape. "That is so rare," I remember Dan saying. There was nothing left of one side except for the trunk. I took a penknife out and carved words into the trunk. Such a distinct memory.

I wander closer and see the words:

'Lovesong

Think of me

Always'

And underneath, are more:

'If only

you'd come

Dan

X'

THE END.

'Then Neither Do I' was published in CafeLit in 2020.

2. Then Neither Do I

Wordcount: 479

There's always a danger in prostitution, but I'd experienced nothing like this before. The aggressiveness of the blow took me by surprise. My dress fell off my shoulder, and I threw out my arms to catch my fall.

As if in slow motion, the stony ground beneath me inched into vision. Closer and closer. And then I hit the floor.

My arm felt the impact. Scraped skin. Possibly a broken bone.

Before I had a chance to think, David's foot flashed before my eyes and rammed into my stomach, stealing my breath.

His wife found out he'd been buying my favours, and his response was to take it out on me. He claimed I had tempted him away from the sanctity of marriage.

"Whore!" David spat at me. I looked up. His piercing eyes full of venom; nose scrunched; lips curled in hatred. "We all know the punishment for adultery, don't we!"

Being stoned to death was one of the most brutal things I'd witnessed, and I'd seen my fair share of violence. An alcoholic dad set me up with a thorough knowledge of what men were capable of. I'd felt the back of his hand across my face on many occasions. And worse.

A kick to my mouth split open my lip, and a fountain of blood sprayed across the gravelly road. I laid there, too scared to move.

I could hear the movement of footsteps around me; the muttering of male voices, condemning, judging, hating. Then it went quiet.

I heard the accusing voice of one of the religious leaders: "So what should we do with her? This woman has been caught committing adultery!"

Hesitantly, I turned to see what was happening and another man stepped closer towards me. Someone I didn't recognise. He moved slowly. His hair long and dark, his beard thick, his eyes looking down in a thoughtful expression. He bent down next to me and put his finger to the ground. Small stones and dust leapt upwards as he moved his hand through the sandy ground, writing something. In the quietness, the crunch of this motion was deafening.

Then he stood up.

He spoke in a quiet, low voice: "Whoever is without sin, throw the first stone."

Silence.

A small rock landed with a thud on the ground nearby.

And another.

Lots of stones dropping onto the harsh gravel path. And then the sound of footsteps, walking away.

I looked up through swollen eyes. The man's hand was reaching towards me. A strong hand; covered in scars; small cuts that you might see on a carpenter. I raised mine towards his and felt the touch.

Effortlessly and gently, he pulled me to my feet.

His hazel eyes glistened with life; serene; divine.

"Where are your accusers? Has no-one condemned you?"

The street was empty.

"No-one." I managed to whisper.

"Then neither do I."

THE END

'Meeting Kafka' was published by Adelaide literary magazine in December 2020.

3. Meeting Kafka

Wordcount: 2,582

"Morning, I'm calling about the room you've got advertised."

"Sorry, it's already taken."

"Okay, thank you." I drew a line through the phone number on my piece of paper. Another one gone. Surely, I wouldn't end up homeless on my first day at university.

My family weren't interested in helping. "What

are you wasting your money on that for? You should be finding yourself a rich man to take care of you." That's the reaction I received from my dad when I told him about my offer from Exeter. He had no interest in encouraging me, with my 'highfalutin ideas' and I had to make my way here this morning by myself, on the National Express coach. The Student Union gave me a list of potential accommodation, but they all proved unsuccessful.

All, that is, except one. It would take two bus journeys to get there but had a sea-view. Without any alternatives, I went to see it.

The three-story house stood alone at the end of a sandy dirt-track. The landlady, Mrs. Johnston, looked to be in her forties, dark, deep-set eyes, auburn hair gathered at the back and secured at the top of her head with a butterfly clip. She wore expensive looking clothes over her full figure. A widow who didn't hide the fact that she needed a lodger.

She greeted me warmly and spoke of the house's many conveniences: the AGA oven, the washing machine I could use whenever required, cost of electricity and gas included. The only potential issue might be the size of the bedroom. Upon inspection, it became apparent I would have to look elsewhere. A single bed took up the majority of floor space and there wasn't even room for a desk.

Mrs. Johnston told me of a room downstairs that a man kept all year round for a discounted rate, and mainly used during the summer. "He might offer it up during the academic months. It's a very good size."

I thanked her for her enthusiasm in finding a solution but told her I would try elsewhere.

Sitting in the university canteen that afternoon, concerned about where I was going to stay, I received a phone call from Mrs. Johnston. The man who rented the downstairs room had agreed to give it up during term time. "I knew it would be no bother. He's very kind. He's currently in London and won't need the room until June, should you want it."

I moved in that evening.

A wooden door opened up into a huge space with high-reaching ceilings and white painted walls. Wooden floorboards stretched the expanse of the area leading to tall patio doors, where the back garden was faintly visible through muslin curtains. Picture frames hung on the walls with prints by Edward Hopper and Magritte. Amongst various pieces of oak furniture, a king-sized brass bed took up one corner and in another stood a shelving unit holding dozens of books. Despite the owner's personality stamped everywhere, it matched my taste. I moved in without changing a thing. Even the pictures were to my liking.

A knock at the door interrupted my thoughts and Mrs. Johnston peered in. "He's a poet."

"Sorry?"

"You're studying literature, aren't you?"

"That's right."

"Well, Kafka, the gentleman whose room you've got, is a published poet. Been renting here for five years. Lovely fellow. He'd do anything for anybody."

"Kafka?"

"His parents named him after Franz Kafka."

"Kafka?" I paused. "I'm familiar with him." The previous summer, I had had a poem published in a magazine. It was printed at the bottom of a page in small writing, and above it was one of his. His name stood out. The editor had commented on how both poems expressed similar emotions, which lead him to place them together.

Mrs. Johnston raised her eyebrows. "Well, there you go. He's a little dreamy." She smiled. "But that's poets for you."

"Dreamy?"

"Like I said, artists are funny folk. I saw him wandering round the garden one night. Must have been about three in the morning, lost in thought. Anyway, I'll leave you be."

Intrigued by the enigmatic character, who's room I inhabited, I browsed the books lining his shelves. Near the bottom I spied his name on a spine and lifted out a short collection of his poems. With special attentiveness, I read his verse:

"As winter howls with driving rain,
I roam the lonely hills again.
In secret pleasure, secret tears,
My vision of you disappears."

I read on through beautiful, lonely sentences. Words that I would have loved to have written myself, and being here by the coastal hills, they felt particularly poignant.

Despite the long distance to the university, I enjoyed my time in the house. My landlady often cooked me meals: Homemade soups, beef casseroles, sometimes washed down with a glass or two of red wine. I also appreciated the chance to wander up on the heath or along the beach when the fancy took me.

I loved studying the Romantics and immersed myself in Blake and Shelley, Byron and Coleridge. Mrs. Johnston shared my interest in literature and we often discussed them over dinner, but for both of us, none of them held quite the same fascination as the man whose room I inhabited. Every now and then I would see one of his poems in a magazine, and Mrs. Johnston would speak of him: "He would often wander in here and hand me one of his new poems, written on the back of an envelope or something similar. I'm sure you'd find him interesting. He's very shy though. Spends most of his time reading or writing and doesn't see many people. Such a lovely young man too. You don't meet many like him."

"I've read his work, but I've never seen him. What does he look like?"

"Some might call him attractive. Some might not. There's a photo of him in the wooden frame on the dresser in your bedroom."

I paused in thought. "That's a Man Ray picture."

"Yes, but he's behind it. When he agreed to let out his room, he told me to cover it up. 'I don't want anyone looking at me and I'm sure she wouldn't want me staring at her.' So, I put the Man Ray over the top. If you take it out, you'll see him underneath."

When I got back to my room, I re-read one of his poems. One that captured his vulnerability and intensity:

"My heart longs for a touch divine,
And for another soul to find
Me here, beside the wild sea,
To cherish and to comfort me."

I picked up the picture-frame, removed the back, and set it on the dresser. It was a striking image. Dark hair combed back but slightly thinning, sideburns down to the collar of a leather jacket that covered the bottom of his chin. Hazel eyes looked out without giving anything away, like a character from an Edward Hopper painting. Here was the man who expressed thoughts and feelings that I identified with, in ways nobody else seemed able to.

I read his whole volume of work and learned some of his poems by heart. I tried to emulate his style in my own writing, but no matter how hard I tried, couldn't get close. The more I read, the more my fascination grew, intensified by living in his environment, and topped off with information from our mutual landlady.

One evening, a tapping sound alerted me to Mrs. Johnston by the door. "Sorry to bother you." She held a long, dark overcoat in her hands. "It belongs to Kafka. Would you mind keeping it in the wardrobe for me?"

"No, not at all." She placed it into my arms and left me to put it away.

I held it close and breathed in the musky aftershave scent. When I put it in the wardrobe, something fell to the floor. A small notebook patterned in black and red roses. It contained scribblings and doodles, ideas and reflections. Sitting on the bed, I read through them. Half-finished verses spoke of solitude and loneliness and a need for deep connection. I wondered if I'd ever meet Kafka.

***

At the end of the first term of university, some friends on my course told me of a room going in their house. One of their friends had dropped out and left a vacant place. When I mentioned this to Mrs. Johnston, she let out a small gasp and put her hand over her chest. She composed herself. "Do what feels right for you."

That evening, I noticed some faint writing on the wall by the side of my bed. When Mrs. Johnston called at my room to ask if I wanted any food, I pointed it out to her. "Here. I'm surprised I didn't notice it before."

She stepped into the room and climbed onto the bed to get a closer look. "It looks like the beginnings of a poem. He probably woke one night and wrote his ideas down before he forgot them."

"I think you're right."

Mrs. Johnston started to read them out:

"My darling pain, both day and night,
You are my intimate delight."

That night I couldn't sleep. After glancing at the scribblings again, I got out of bed. A silvery light shone through the ghost-like curtains, and I walked over to the door. I pulled back the drapes and looked into the garden. The bright moon gave the world a strange grey hue. I turned the key slowly so as not to wake anyone and stepped outside. The clear air was perfectly still. I stepped onto the lawn, and with the dewy grass clinging to my feet, made my way towards the shadowed woodland at the end of the garden.

Such a beautiful night.

A small creature scuttled over the grass in front of me and disappeared into the undergrowth. Leaves stirred on the bushes, and I turned to look back at the house. Part of me wanted to leave and be with my friends in the hive of student activity, but another part felt an immense connection with the poet and this building. I stood a while and was about to go back when I noticed a dark figure move through the trees and disappear into the blackness.

Kafka? He wouldn't be here, surely. He was in London.

There again, further on, a man walked towards the beach. I could hear the gentle roll of waves, and watched him sit down on the sand, facing the sea. His hands supported his body as he leaned back. Who was he? What was he doing out at this time? I stood for a while, watching.

The tide came in on a strong current and washed under him, but he stayed where he sat. Taking a deep breathe, he tilted his head back into the night sky. A cloud covered the moon and he glanced around. My heart raced, I pulled back into the shadows, and headed back to my room.

***

I decided to stay at the house. My friends couldn't understand why, but I told them I enjoyed the beach and the home-cooked meals too much. Deep down, I always knew I wouldn't leave.

Blood Ink magazine published one of my poems, along with three other previously unpublished writers, and to my surprise and delight, Kafka, being a regular contributor to the magazine, reviewed them. He wrote that mine was sensitive and moving and showed promise of more to come. The magazine printed another of his pieces alongside mine and my longing to meet him overpowered any other ambition.

I took advantage of the email address printed next to his name and wrote to him. I thanked him for his review, expressed my admiration for his work, and informed him that by strange coincidence, I temporarily resided in his room.

When I told Mrs Johnston this, she showed palpable excitement. "You've got a real soft spot for him, haven't you?" She smiled. "Let me know if you hear back from him."

That night, I placed Kafka's picture on my bedside cabinet and scanned the scribblings on the wall. While I reclined on my bed, I spoke out my favorite lines from his poetry, warm and sweet as they brushed my lips.

"With a tender heart, I swore
To give my spirit to adore
You, ever present, phantom being,

My slave, my poet, and my queen."

Now I lay where he had, my face on the pillow where he had slept, immersed in his presence.

An email from him the following day elated me. Kafka expressed a genuine enthusiasm for my poem, delight that I had been the person who took on his room, and a promise to look out for more of my contributions in the future. Mrs. Johnston advised me to continue with the correspondence and showed a real interest in my feelings for him. "You know, you'd make a lovely couple."

The emails continued between myself and Kafka daily, and one Friday, he informed me that he would be calling in at the house to collect some books. He wrote that he looked forward to catching up with Mrs. Johnston and meeting me in person.

That morning, I chose my clothes carefully. A

70

pale pink top and jeans that fit particularly well.

The curtains moved gently with the morning breeze; the waves audible in the distance. Mid-morning, a knock at the front-door informed me of a visitor. I waited a few minutes and then, unable to stay in my room any longer, stepped into the hallway.

Mrs. Johnston closed the front-door and turned towards me. "Oh, you're going to be so disappointed. Kafka changed his mind. I'm sorry. I know how much you were looking forward to meeting him."

"He changed his mind?"

"He called, but decided against coming in. Headed into town instead at the last minute. He's not been doing great to be honest with you. His last collection of poetry got slated in a review recently and he really took it to heart. Too raw and passionate is how the poems were criticized. It really got to him. The problem is he spends so long by himself that he has the time to dwell on that kind of thing."

"He was here?"

"He was. He's just not up to socializing at the moment."

I rushed forward and opened the door. I descended the steps and looked down the street but there was no sign of him. I had come so close. Would I get the opportunity again?

"He's gone." I told Mrs. Johnston.

"I'm sorry." She held my arm, and our eyes connected. She would be ready to console me should I need her.

I returned to my room and immersed myself in Kafka's words. Surely our paths would cross eventually.

Racing thoughts prevented me from sleeping that night.

"And reason mocks my muddled thoughts,
That deaden me to real cares."

***

Two days later, sitting at the kitchen table, I glanced over at the paper:

"SUICIDE WITH EXETER CONNECTION."

I puller the paper closer:

"The body of up-and-coming poet, Kafka, was discovered yesterday afternoon. He had begun to receive international recognition for his sensitive and moving poetry but was found dead in his London apartment. Next to his body was found a collection of unpublished works. His latest collection, 'To An Unknown Woman', had just been released.

THE END

'Into The Lonely Night' was published by Friday Flash Fiction in January 2021.

.

4. Into the Lonely Night

Wordcount: 99

I saw you this evening.

You were standing on the other side of the German market by the wooden nativity scene. The neon star's aura shone over the long cream coat I bought you last Christmas.

"Lulu!" My attempt was drowned out by bustling customers and Nat King Cole crooning 'Unforgettable' through nearby speakers.

Frantically, I squeezed through the crowd; enveloped by the smell of damp clothes, mulled wine, and cinnamon.

Just as I reached the path, breathless, I caught a glimpse of your hand closing the taxi door, and watched the rear lights disappear into the lonely night.

THE END.

'Blondie' was published by the audio podcast Tall Tale TV in January 2021.

6. BLONDIE

Wordcount: 1, 608

A knock at my bedroom door startles me. Greg, one of my housemates, pokes his head in. "Would you do me a favour? I need someone to come on a double-date."

"Who's it with?"

"Susie and her mate from the art class. She's supposed to be hot."

"Is she blonde?"

Greg shakes his head. "Man, what is it with you and blondes?"

If I tell him the truth, he won't believe me. Not many people would. There's a good reason for it though. It all goes back to my last day of school.

I was talking to my classmate, Haruki, on the walk home. Approaching the top of Bleak Hill, about a quarter of a mile from my house, sunlight spilled across the road and a warm breeze carried the scent of Yoshino cherries.

Haruki kicked a battered Coke can across the street. "I can't believe this is our last day."

I pulled the straps of my backpack tighter. "I know, it's a real anti-climax. I guess things will be different from now on though."

And then it happened. The road before me swayed, my head throbbed, and the houses rotated around me. My pace slackened, and Haruki turned to look at me. "Are you all right?"

I squatted on the pavement and closed my eyes. When I opened them I was in a kitchen. There was a wooden table, and on it, a greeting card. It was black with the words: 'Happy 20th Anniversary'.

I turned my head and examined the rest of the room. A woman bent down to take a dish from an oven. The smell of roast lamb wafted over. A strand of blonde hair fell over her face, and her eyes met mine. Beautiful, dark blue eyes.

A white mist closed in around me, and I was back, squatting on the pavement. The spring breeze brushed my face, and birds called to one another from the surrounding trees.

Haruki's face came into view with furrowed eyebrows. "Dan?"

"I was in a house with a woman and...it was so real."

***

If that had been the only time it occurred, it might not have had such an impact. I would have put it down to a wild imagination and the stress of exams or sleep-deprivation, but a few weeks after I started university, a similar thing happened.

I shared a house with three guys in a rough part of the city where the rent was cheap. Coming home one evening, as I pushed open the door, I felt dizzy, like I'd stood up too fast. I went to my room, sat on the bed, and closed my eyes. When I opened them, I was standing in an unfamiliar hallway. Just as before, I had no idea where I was, although felt strangely at home.

Light shone through a frosted glass transom.

A patterned Minton tile floor led to a staircase on my right, two wooden doors on my left, and another at the end of the hall. A peaceful ambience soothed me: the smell of polished wood and steady tick-tock of an antique clock.

I stepped through the nearest doorway into a living room. A blue sofa stood against one wall across from a fireplace with a Victorian brass register and marble surround. Shelves of books filled each side: Picasso, Nancy Spero, Art at the Turn of the 21st Century.

A photograph leaned against the wall on the windowsill. It was the blonde woman. She looked younger though. Stunning. Her hair pulled behind her head, one strand hanging over her face, and a slight shadow under her cheekbones. She wore a khaki vest and a circular pendant hung from a black string around her neck. A child rested on her hip, maybe two years old with a finger in his mouth, looking towards the camera with oval blue eyes.

I put the photo back.

"Dan? Are you okay?" a feminine voice with a slight Irish lilt called from the hall.

I hesitantly stepped back to the doorway and looked up the stairs.

"Are you coming?" she asked.

A white haze closed in, and I was back on my bed in my student room. I took a deep breath; sweat beaded on my brow. I had no idea what was going on.

Fearing the story would be the target for merriment, I didn't speak to anyone about it. There was no one I trusted enough. So, despite being disturbed and also intrigued, I carried on as normal and settled into a routine of breakfast, lectures, lunch in the canteen, and research in the library.

In April, I was strolling home through Aston

Park. It was the kind of day where you're not sure if you need an umbrella; the dampness in the air bringing out the scent of the earth. An uncomfortable pressure pounded in my head. Sunlight broke through leaves swaying above me, flickering orange and white.

I blinked, and a silhouette of the blonde woman moved before me, daylight shining through lead-framed windows behind her. We were in a living room with white walls and wooden floorboards.

I smelled the fresh pine of a Christmas tree and had a bauble in my hand ready to place on a branch.

"Do you remember this?" She smiled and held up a wooden model house with snow painted on its roof.
I looked at it, hanging from her fingertips, and then at her face. I held her gaze, dark blue with flecks of brown and grey, full lips curved down at the corners with a confident charm.

Her forehead creased. "Are you okay?"

"Yeah." I smiled, and then a mist moved in around me, and I was back, walking through the park.

***

Greg holds his hand up like he's about to launch into an operatic song. "Come on man. She might be blonde. Whatever. It'll be a craic."

"When is it?"

"Tonight."
"I've got a test tomorrow."

"Come on Dan. I'm desperate. Susie won't come unless I bring someone else."

I smile at the hopelessness in his voice. "Okay, I'll come."

"Awesome. We need to leave at nine. Be ready by then, yeah?"

My heart starts to pound. Could it be the woman from my strange visions? Does she even exist?

After the dreamlike experiences, I went to the university library to research what the cause of it might be. I found a book in the Medical Section called 'Conditions That Are As Bizarre As They Are Fascinating'. Inside, I discovered Chrono-Lapse Syndrome. A rare genetic disorder. It causes the afflicted to jump through time at unpredictable moments and remain there, sometimes for just a few seconds, sometimes for hours. I became convinced I had the condition.

I started looking out for the blonde woman in real time. Every day, I scanned the faces of people on the city streets of Birmingham or in bars when I was out with friends. Always wondering when, or if, we would meet.

Two months later, I was sitting at my bedroom desk, revising for an end-of-term test. A table lamp lit a pile of books in front of me. The light began to dazzle me, and I felt that same light-headed sensation. The familiar haze closed in, and when I regained my vision, green and rusty coloured hills stretched before me, with a narrow dirt track leading to the sea.

Overhead, seagulls cried from a cloudless sky. I breathed in the clean, salty air. The woman stood on a small wooden bridge two hundred meters away. The wind blew her pale green dress around her thighs.

I shouted: "Hey, Blondie!"

She looked my direction, then skipped away towards the beach. I followed.

Waves crashed into rocks, and fine spray drifted through the air.

"Come on!" she shouted over the roar of the sea, beckoning me to a rock she stood against.

I stepped across the stones and sat next to her.
She held a camera out and pointed it towards us. She grinned. "What a beautiful honeymoon."

The shutter clicked, and the bright light of my table lamp reappeared. My university notes came back into focus. I shook my head, wishing I could return.

Blondie mesmerized me. I couldn't entertain the idea of being with anyone else.

***

At 9: 45, Greg and I step off the bus onto one of the busy streets of Birmingham. Groups of young people pass by, shouting and laughing loudly under the drizzly autumn sky.

"This way!" Greg beckons. Bright lights from streetlamps reflect off wet pavements. Doormen with their arms folded, stand outside venues with thumping dance music.

"Susie!" Greg approaches two girls standing outside a pub entrance. One holds an umbrella over their heads, and the other stands shivering, with her hands in her back pockets.

"Dan!" Greg motions with his hand. "This is Susie and...?" He looks at his date.

"Lacy."

Susie raises the umbrella, revealing more of her friend. Red lipstick, warm brown eyes, dark curly hair. My shoulders sag.

"Hi." I try to force a sincere smile.

Red and yellow lights behind them flash to the music, reflecting on the pub wall. My head throbs, and the white mist closes in.

I'm lying in a bed, naked, with Blondie next to me. Her head rests on me, hair spilt across my chest. Sunlight streams in through a gap in the curtains, illuminating specks of dust in the air. I have no idea where I am, but I don't care. I breathe in the scent of Blondie's skin and place my hand on her shoulder. I'm convinced I'll meet her soon.

THE END

'Familiar Eyes' was published by Friday Flash Fiction and Bright Flash Literary Review in 2020.

4. Familiar Eyes

Wordcount: 883

A fierce downpour pounded the pavement outside Birmingham International Airport and lashed against my windscreen. The rear lights of the car in front lit up, and a cloud of exhaust fumes gusted into the night air. Through the dissipating smoke I saw her walking towards me, dressed in a red coat and woollen hat. She placed a case on the pavement next to my cab.

I stepped outside, keeping my face down, away from the bitter rain. "Taxi?"

"Yes, please. Western Road." My last fare of the night.

Something about her accent reminded me of someone as I opened the door to let her in.

I started the engine and tried to put a face to the distinctive voice. "Been anywhere nice?"

In my rear-view mirror, I watched as her brow creased in thought and she removed her hat. "Ireland," she said, and it clicked.

"Lulu."

We were a couple, fifteen years ago. That unmistakable Irish lilt brought me back to student days, gigs, drunkenly stumbling around cheap student accommodation, talking and smoking into the early hours.

"Dan." She smiled.

"How are you?"

"I'm okay." She paused a moment, then continued. "I'm back for a book signing tomorrow."

"A book-signing? That's great." She had aspirations of being a writer when we were at university. "Poetry?" She never stopped writing poems. In notebooks, on scraps of paper, on her hands, wherever she was, whenever she thought of it.

"It's a novel," she said.

"What's it called?"

She hesitated. "Meeting Bronte."

Wuthering Heights was our favourite book. We visited Emily Bronte's house together and spent a weekend camping on the Howarth moor where the story was set.

"Sounds interesting. I'll have to get a copy."

Memories flooded over me like the ephemeral raindrops dashing against my windscreen. The light from headlights glided over the inside of the car.

Our relationship had been intense and unpredictable, joyful yet exhausting. It ended when she returned to Ireland to 'get her head straight', leaving me devastated.

"I wrote to you." she whispered.

I glanced in my mirror and saw her beautiful dark familiar eyes. "Yeah, I got your poem, but you didn't put a return address on."

"I put it on the letters."

"The letters?"

"I sent you letters but you didn't reply."

I took a deep breath. "The lease ran out on my house shortly after you left. I didn't get any letters. I did call in every now and then to ask if anything had come but the new tenants weren't interested."

Her eyes widened.

"I tried looking you up," I said, "but I didn't know which village you were from."

We were silent for a few minutes, the windscreen wipers clearing the raindrops that distorted my view. In the rear-view mirror I saw shadows move across her face.

"How have you been?" she asked. "Are you married?"

"No. You?"

"I'm going through a divorce." She looked outside at the passing city landscape.

"Sorry to hear that." I said, as I pulled onto the expressway.

"What have you been doing? Weren't you thinking of going into the ministry?"

"Yeah, I was a vicar up in Ayr for seven years."

"I bet you did a wonderful job."

"It's a difficult role. I'm on a break at the moment. It's lasted about five years so far." I paused. "I went to the Wuthering Heights pub."

She would know what I was referring to. When we stayed in Haworth, I asked her to meet me back there on my thirtieth birthday at midnight, whether we were together or not. I returned but she didn't.

"I know" she said.

"You know?"

"I went at midnight on the night of your birthday. It was only afterwards that I realised you returned on the turn of midnight on the morning. That's why we missed each other. I saw your message on the tree but had no way of finding you."

Under an inscription of some words, she had carved on our first visit, I had written:

'IF ONLY

YOU'D COME

DAN

X'

***

She opened her purse and asked if she could smoke.

"It's not allowed; but feel free."

I saw the end of the cigarette burning in the shadows and smoke filled the cab. She opened her window a little. "Do you want one?"

"Yeah, thanks."

She handed me the cigarette she'd already lit, just like the old days. I took a deep drag and felt the nicotine rush to my head. I blew the smoke out. "It's been a while."

"I've been trying to give up." she said.

As I pulled up to her house, I told her I was glad we'd run into each other. She opened her purse and pulled out a fifty-pound note for the twenty-pound fare. "Thanks for the lift."

I went to give her change but she held up her hand in protest. Was she trying to communicate something? Was it an apology?

"Thanks," I said.

I watched her walk down the path to her house. She went inside without looking back.

I held up the fifty-pound note, and in the corner was a telephone number and a name, Lulu.

THE END

'Probably Not For The Likes Of Me' was the winner of the annual Friday Flash Fiction Christmas Competition in 2020.

5. Probably not for the likes of me

Wordcount: 91

The fire crackles and I place more wood into the flames. Orange light flickers over her face as she sleeps. So beautiful, but pregnant, and the baby's not mine.

Smoke rises into the air, and I sit back, looking into the clear night sky.

I must admit, the star everyone is talking about is impressive. They say it's a sign that a change is going to come. Probably not for the likes of me though.

Looking down the hill, in the distance I can just make out the lights of Bethlehem.

THE END

'Purple Rain' is a shortened amalgamation of 'Waiting For Lulu at Wuthering Heights' and 'Lovesong', written from Dan's point of view.

It was published Spillwords, Friday Flash Fiction, and River City Tree.

7. Purple Rain

Wordcount: 493

A pound coin

       clatters

          down

            the slot.

I scroll through the song choices and punch in 6-2-4. A seven-inch record of Prince's 'Purple Rain' moves into position.

The tonearm slides across the vinyl disc and there's a CRACKLE as the needle settles

into   grooves.
        the

A melancholy guitar chord erupts from the speakers. The familiar steady rhythm and haunting vocals begin, stirring my gut.

I'm in The Angel on New Year's Eve, a pub Lulu and I frequented in the early nineties. It's a lonely place to be by myself. I go back to my seat, undo the top button of my shirt, remove my Anglican clerical collar and place it on the table.

I feel twenty again.

The place hasn't changed. It still has the same decor: oak beams, lead windows, black walls with torn posters of The Charlatans and

The Stone Roses, the smell of ale and
                         stagnant
                                         smoke.

I glance at the door and imagine Lulu walking
in. It's been eight years since I've seen her.

As 'Purple Rain' plays on, I take out a photo
of her. There's a white fold line across the
middle of the picture but it's the only one I
have. It's from her student house in Leeds.
Her eyes, wild and dark, stare back. Her skin
is unblemished with naturally pink cheeks.
Blonde cropped hair hangs long at the front,
blunt cut to her jawline on one side. I place
the photo on the table next to my collar.

Out the window, snowflakes

        tumble

      in

ever-changing

courses.

Fleeting shapes

fall

and

disintegrate

on the glass

before my eyes can catch them,

and I'm lost in memories of her again.

***

Sitting outside the tent, a short distance from here, under the cloudless blue sky, we took in the endless moors and breathed the sweet summer air.

'Purple Rain' came on the battered stereo that I had brought along. Lulu pulled me to my feet, and we danced, close. Her dark blue eyes met mine.

"When you hear this song, think of me."

I wanted to ask her to marry me, but I was scared she'd turn me down. Instead, I asked, "Do you think we'll still be together when we're in our thirties?"

"Maybe," her eyes crinkled, amused at my question.

And then, to ensure we didn't lose contact, I came up with this ridiculous idea: "Let's meet back at the Angel on New Year's Eve in the year 2000, no matter what. At midnight."

"Okay." She smiled.

***

A glance at my watch tells me it's ten past twelve. I place my collar and photo in my pocket and step outside into the cold night air.

There's no sign of anyone. The moon is big and bright. It's stopped snowing and the wind has died down. Everything is white. I pull my coat collar tight around my neck and look towards the hills where Lulu and I camped. I pause for a moment and hold my breath. In the distance, a figure stands motionless with a dog by their side.

Lulu?

I step closer. All I can hear is my own

breathing and the light crunch of each step as I move forward. The dog breaks free and a man shouts something incomprehensible.

A warm tear

rolls

down

my

cold face.

THE END

'Meeting Bronte' is an alternative version of 'Meeting Kafka'. It tells the story from a male perspective and the ending is different.

It was published by Ariel Chart Review, Pif magazine, and Fiction On The Web.

9. Meeting Bronte

Wordcount: 2, 517

"Morning, I'm calling about the room you've got advertised."

"Sorry, it's already taken."

"Okay, thank you." I drew a line through the phone number on my piece of paper. Another one gone. Surely, I wouldn't end up homeless on my first day at university.

I had spent the summer working as a waiter at a holiday resort in America and hadn't been able to view any properties during the weeks leading up to my first year. The Student Union had given me a list of potential places that morning, but they all proved unsuccessful.

All, that is, except one. It would take two bus journeys to get there but had a sea-view. Without any alternative, I went to see it.

The three-story house stood alone at the end of a sandy dirt-track. The landlady, Mrs Johnston, looked to be in her forties, with auburn hair gathered at the back and secured at the top of her head with a butterfly clip. She wore expensive looking clothes over her full figure. A widow who didn't hide the fact that she needed a lodger. She greeted me warmly and spoke of the house's many conveniences: the AGA oven, the washing machine I could use whenever required, cost of electricity and gas included. The only potential issue might be the size of the bedroom. Upon inspection, it became apparent I would have to look elsewhere. A single bed took up the majority of floor space and there wasn't even room for a desk.

Mrs. Johnston told me of a room downstairs that a woman kept all year round for a discounted rate, and mainly used during the summer. "She might offer it up during the academic months. It's a very good size."

I thanked her for her enthusiasm in finding a solution but told her I would try elsewhere.

Sitting in the university canteen, worried about where I was going to stay that night, I received a phone call from Mrs. Johnston. The woman who rented the downstairs room had agreed to give it up during term time. "I knew it would be no bother. She's very kind. She's currently in London and won't need the room until June, should you want it."

I moved in that evening.

A wooden door opened up into a huge space with high-reaching ceilings and white painted walls. Wooden floorboards stretched the expanse of the area leading to tall patio doors, where the back garden was faintly visible through muslin curtains. Picture frames hung on the walls with prints by Edward Hopper and Magritte. Amongst various pieces of oak furniture, a king-sized brass bed took up one corner and in another stood a shelving unit holding dozens of books. Despite the owner's personality stamped everywhere, it matched my taste. I moved in without changing a thing. Even the pictures were to my liking.

A knock at the door interrupted my thoughts and Mrs. Johnston peered in. "She's a poet."

"Sorry?"

"You're studying literature, aren't you?"

"That's right."

"Well, Brontë, the woman whose room you've got, is a published poet. Been renting here for five years. Lovely lady. She'd do anything for anybody."

"Brontë?"

"Her parents named her after Emily Brontë."

"Brontë, the poet?" I paused. "I'm familiar with her." I had had a poem published in a magazine the previous summer. It was printed at the bottom of a page in small writing, and above it was one of hers. Her name stood out. The editor had commented on how both poems expressed similar emotions, which lead him to place them together.

Mrs. Johnston raised her eyebrows. "Well, there you go. She's a little dreamy." She smiled. "But that's poets for you."

"Dreamy?"

"Like I said, artists are funny folk. I saw her wandering round the garden one night. Must have been about three in the morning, lost in thought. Anyway, I'll leave you be."

Intrigued by the enigmatic character, who's room I inhabited, I browsed the books lining her shelves. Near the bottom I spied her name on a spine and lifted out a short collection of her poems. With special attentiveness, I read her verse:

"As winter howls with driving rain,
I roam the lonely hills again.
In secret pleasure, secret tears,
My vision of you disappears."

I read on through beautiful, lonely sentences. Words that I would have loved to have written myself; and being here on the edge of the coastal hills, they felt particularly poignant.

Despite the long distance to the university, I

enjoyed my time in the house. My landlady often cooked me meals: Homemade soups, beef casseroles, sometimes washed down with a glass or two of red wine. I also appreciated the chance to wander up on the heath or along the beach when the fancy took me.

I loved studying the Romantics and immersed myself in Blake and Shelley, Byron and Coleridge. Mrs Johnston shared my interest in literature and we often discussed them over dinner, but for both of us, none of them held quite the same fascination as the woman whose room I inhabited. Every now and then I would see one of her poems in a magazine, and Mrs Johnston would speak of her: "She used to walk in the kitchen, mid-morning, and put the coffee on. She would often hand me one of her new poems, written on the back of an envelope or something similar. I'm sure you'd find her interesting. She's very shy though. Spends most of her time reading or writing and doesn't see many people. Such a lovely young lady too. You don't meet many like her."

"I've read her work, but I've never seen her. What does she look like?"

"Some might call her attractive. Some might not. There's a photo of her in the wooden frame on the dresser in your bedroom."

I paused in thought. "That's a Man Ray picture."

"Yes, but she's behind it. When she agreed to let out her room, she told me to cover it up. 'I don't want anyone looking at me and I'm sure he wouldn't want me staring at him.' So, I put the Man Ray over the top. If you take it out, you'll see her underneath."

When I got back to my room, I re-read one of her poems. One that captured her vulnerability and intensity:

"My heart longs for a touch divine,
And for another soul to find
Me here, beside the wild sea,
To cherish and to comfort me."

I picked up the picture-frame, removed the back, and set it on the dresser. It was a striking image. Rusty coloured hair hung down the sides of her face contrasting with a turquoise scarf around her neck. Dark blue eyes looked up thoughtfully, like a character from an Edward Hopper painting. Here was the woman who expressed thoughts and feelings that I identified with, in ways nobody else seemed able to.

Beautiful.

I read her whole volume of work and learned some of her poems by heart. I tried to emulate her style in my own writing, but no matter how hard I tried, couldn't get close. The more I read, the more my fascination grew, intensified by living in her environment, and topped off with information from our mutual landlady.

One evening, a tapping sound alerted me to Mrs. Johnston by the door. "Sorry to bother you." She held an olive green, woolen coat in her hands. "It belongs to Brontë. Would you mind keeping it in the wardrobe for me?"

"No, not at all." She placed it into my arms and left me to put it away.

I held it close and breathed in the scent of perfume on the collar. When I put it in the wardrobe, something fell to the floor. A small notebook; patterned in black and pink roses. It contained scribblings and doodles, ideas and reflections. Sitting on the bed, I read through them. Half-finished verses spoke of solitude and loneliness and a need for deep connection. I wondered if I'd ever meet Brontë.

***

At the end of the first term of university, some friends on my course told me of a room going in their house. One of their mates had dropped out and left a vacant place.

That evening, I noticed some faint writing on the wall by the side of my bed. When Mrs. Johnston called at my room to ask if I wanted any food, I pointed it out to her. "Here. I'm surprised I didn't notice it before."

She stepped into the room. "It looks like the beginnings of a poem. She probably woke one night and wrote her ideas down before she forgot them."

"I think you're right."

Mrs. Johnston read them out:

"My darling pain, both day and night,
You are my intimate delight."

That night I couldn't sleep. After glancing at the scribblings again, I got out of bed. A silvery light shone through the ghost-like curtains, and I walked over to the door. I pulled back the drapes and looked into the garden. The bright moon gave the world a strange grey hue. I turned the key slowly so as not to wake anyone and stepped outside. The clear air was perfectly still. I stepped onto the lawn, and with the dewy grass clinging to my feet, made my way towards the shadowed woodland at the end of the garden.

Such a beautiful night.

A small creature scuttled over the grass in front of me and disappeared into the undergrowth. Leaves stirred on the bushes, and I turned to look back at the house. Part of me wanted to leave and be with my friends in the hive of student activity, but another part felt an immense connection with the poet and this building. I stood a while and was about to go back when I noticed a dark figure move through the trees and disappear into the blackness.

Brontë? She wouldn't be here, surely. She was in London.

There again, further on, a woman wearing a thin white gown walked towards the beach. I could hear the gentle roll of waves, and watched her sit down on the sand, facing the sea. Her hands supported her body as she leaned back. Who was she? What was she doing out at this time? I stood for a while, watching.

The tide came in on a strong current and washed under her, but she stayed where she sat. Taking a deep breathe, she tilted her head back into the night sky. A cloud covered the moon and she glanced around. My heart raced, I pulled back into the shadows, and headed back to my room.

***

I decided to stay at the house. My friends couldn't understand why, but I told them I enjoyed the beach and the home-cooked meals too much. Deep down, I always knew I wouldn't leave.

Blood Ink magazine published one of my poems, along with three other previously unpublished writers. To my delight, Brontë, being a regular contributor to the magazine, reviewed them. She wrote that mine was sensitive and moving and showed promise of more to come. The magazine printed another of her pieces alongside mine and my longing to meet her overpowered any other ambition.

I took advantage of the email address printed next to her name and wrote to her. I thanked her for her review, expressed my admiration for her work, and informed her that by strange coincidence, I temporarily resided in her room.

When I told Mrs. Johnston this, she showed palpable excitement. "You've got a real soft spot for her, haven't you?" She smiled. "Let me know if you hear back from her."

That night, I placed Brontë's picture on my bedside cabinet and scanned the scribblings on the wall. While I reclined on my bed, I spoke out my favourite lines from her poetry, warm and sweet as they brushed my lips.

"With a ready heart, I swore
To give my spirit to adore
You, ever present, phantom thing,
My slave, my poet, and my king."

Now I lay where she had, my face on the pillow where she had slept, immersed in her presence.

An email from her the following day elated me. Brontë expressed a genuine enthusiasm for my poem, delight that I had been the person who took on her room, and a promise to look out for more of my contributions in the future. Mrs. Johnston advised me to continue with the correspondence. "You know, you'd make a lovely couple."

The emails continued between myself and Brontë daily, and one Friday, she informed me that she would be calling in at the house to collect some books. She wrote that she looked forward to catching up with Mrs. Johnston and meeting me in person.

That morning, I chose my clothes carefully. A checkered red and black shirt that fit particularly well.

The curtains moved gently with the morning breeze; the waves audible in the distance. Mid-morning, a knock at the front-door informed me of a visitor. I waited a few minutes and then, unable to stay in my room any longer, stepped into the hallway.

Mrs. Johnston closed the front-door and turned towards me. "Oh, you're going to be so disappointed. Brontë changed her mind. I'm sorry. I know how much you were looking forward to meeting her."

"She changed her mind?"

"She called, but decided against coming in. Headed into town instead at the last minute. She's not been doing great to be honest with you. Her last collection of poetry got slated in a review recently and she really took it to heart. Too raw and passionate is how the poems were criticized. It really got to her. The problem is she spends so long by herself that she has the time to dwell on that kind of thing."

"She was here?"

"She was. She's just not up to socializing at the moment."

I rushed forward and opened the door. I descended the steps and looked down the street but there was no sign of her. I had come so close. Would I get the opportunity again?

"She's gone." I told Mrs Johnston.

"I'm so sorry."

Racing thoughts prevented me from sleeping that night.

"And reason mocks my muddled thoughts,
That deaden me to real cares."

A solid yellow block of light shone under my bedroom door indicating that Mrs. Johnston was up. She was the only person who understood my feelings for Brontë, and I felt a need to speak with her.

I put on my dressing-gown and stepped into

the hallway. A steaming cup of tea stood on the kitchen table next to a notepad and pencil. She would be back in a moment. I put the kettle back on so I could join her and took a seat. The notepad caught my attention. Poetry. I looked closer to see a message with my name at the top, and at the bottom the name Brontë.

THE END.

Made in the USA
Las Vegas, NV
20 February 2021